MASQUE

OF

HONOR

MASQUE
OF
HONOR

EDWARD LINN
AND
JACK PEARL

W · W · *Norton & Company · Inc* ·
New York

To all our children

MASQUE

OF

HONOR

Walter Bruno, twisting an unlit cigarette in his fingers, stared out the window into the windless, drenching rain falling straight onto the parade grounds. He shared the small room with two other correspondents in the barracks which housed the U. S. press corps.

Fitted into one corner of their cramped quarters was an unfinished door serving as a makeshift desk. Although three typewriters were lined up on top of it, there were only two chairs. Only two reporters could work at the desk with any comfort, at the same time.

Cy Wharton, a thin blond man, was hammering away at his machine, the sound of the clacking keys having the same steady monotonous rhythm as the rain striking on the barracks' metal roof.

Turning from the window Bruno shambled over toward the sound, placed both hands on Coleman's shoulders and bent to read his story.

CALU, South Vietnam, February 17, 1968—A major battle, possibly the most crucial battle of the Vietnam War, is shaping up at the allied military base at Khesanh where 5,000 U. S. Marines and South Vietnamese Rangers are surrounded by 50,000 North Vietnamese regulars and Vietcong forces. The Khesanh base is the western anchor for the allied defense line below the demilitarized zone and blocks five vital arteries that can be used by the enemy to speed men and material from north to south should the base fall. The loss of Khesanh would be a disaster comparable to the loss of Dienbienphu by the French back in 1954. . . ."

"That's a bushel of bullshit, Cy," Bruno snorted. "Khesanh no longer has any real military value to anybody at this point. It's all psychological. They own everything around it, north, south, east, west: What the hell do they need to take the base for? Those poor-bastard Marines might just as well be back in Saigon for all the threat they pose to Charley."

Cy Wharton swung around in the chair, his expression mildly belligerent. "You write your stories, Walt, and I'll write mine, huh? I suppose you think our Marines should put their tails between their legs and run?"

The door was flung open and Adam March strode into the room; a typical March entrance, complete with sound effects. A typical March entrance, with all the presence of an actor coming on stage. March was a dramatic looking figure, dripping water from his green beret and special services uniform. His warlike appearance was enriched by the Colt .45 automatic holstered on his right hip and two hand grenades hooked to his pistol belt.

"The Marines at Khesanh aren't going to run anywhere!" March announced in a voice that cracked with authority. "You can quote me on that, gentlemen!"

Bruno and Wharton grinned as March divested himself

of gun, grenades, green beret, and soggy jacket and draped the items of clothing over the back of his chair to drip dry. Coleman stood up and they both salaamed.

"Adam March, the ambassador plenipotentiary from Broadway," Bruno said solemnly.

"And he get plenny potentiary dere from ole Stonewall," Wharton said, in a pretty good imitation of De Kingfish.

"Yeah," Bruno said. "What's the latest romance in the Mekong Delta, Adam? Tell it like it really is now, are Westmoreland and General Kye going *pffffffhtttt?*"

"Take it from this newsboy," Wharton said, in a quick, high-strung voice that beautifully caricatured March's own crackling delivery, "that the whole Delta is abuzz with rumors about the sizzling romance between Adam March and Old Stonewall Ritter. This newsboy got it straight from an unimpeachable source at the PX that after the last time March whispered sweet nothings into the general's shell-like ear, the general began to polish up a third star."

Through it all, March had been vigorously wiping down his face, neck, and hands. "The Bobbsey twins," he snorted, cleaning out his ears. He flung the towel onto his cot, and favored them with a pleased, secret smile. "I shouldn't give you barracks commandoes anything more than a weather report." He jerked his head toward the window. "It's raining out there," he said, with genial contempt. "You can quote me."

"Not a fit day for man nor beast," Wharton said. He was doing W. C. Fields now, but all the conviction was out of it. "What you got, Adam?"

Ignoring him, March strode to the desk, picked up Wharton's typewriter and set it down to the far end of the desk. He placed his own machine in the center of the desk and sat down. He sandwiched a sheet of carbon between two sheets of canary yellow paper. He ran a hand across his head, smoothing back the close-cropped graying hair. He lit a cigarette, drew deeply, and blew the smoke in the general vicinity of their faces. Dark eyes glittering, he began to type with the concentration of a reporter who is onto something big.

After a few moments, he stopped to reread his lead, pulled the paper out of the carriage, crumpled it in his fist and, without turning, let it drop, not too ostentatiously, at their feet.

Bruno and Wharton were no longer amused.

March was a spare, wiry man with a sharp, angular face. The man was, in fact, all sharp, hard edges, all flint. Everything about him grated against the personalities of his fellow correspondents. Adam March was almost universally disliked among the members of the press corps. He was too flamboyant. Too loud. Too overbearing. Too egotistical. His copy rang with melodrama and ran with purple prose and soap opera. He was, they all agreed, an intolerable human being.

What made him even more infuriating was that they knew he couldn't have cared less what they thought of him. That, in fact, he would have been delighted to know that they spent so much of their time talking about him. For all of his fifty-five years, boy and man, Adam March had taken particular care that people would talk about him.

He would have been a joke, then, if it were not for something inside the man that drew the ridiculous components together into something that was, taken as a whole, impressive. His egotism itself was commanding. The way he had of dominating all press conferences. His utter fearlessness and—at the bottom of it all—his utter confidence that in a roomful of four-star generals, Adam March was the most important person there. He asked stupid, self-serving questions, questions that were sometimes em-

barrassing in their tastelessness and ignorance, but he had
an infallible instinct for homing in on the tough, crucial
questions too. And once he had his teeth in something, he
never let go.

Other reporters might take the position that their read-
ers were entitled to be informed. March's position always
seemed to be that he, Adam March, was omniscient. From
every pore, he radiated the unmistakable attitude that he
made the war itself more important by being there.

That, Cy Wharton had decided, was the thing about
Adam March, all right: his unquestioning confidence in his
own stature in American journalism and, beyond that, his
childlike faith in his own destiny. For better or for worse,
Adam March *was* a figure in American journalism. Despite
their scoffing, the correspondents in Vietnam had buzzed
with excitement at the news that Adam March was on his
way. Cy Wharton himself—blush as he might for it now—
had been mightily pleased to find Adam assigned to his
room in the barracks. He had—God save him—very
quickly written his wife, his brother, and a wide assort-
ment of friends so that he could drop in the information—
purely parenthetically, of course—that he and Adam
March were roommates and, presumably, bosom buddies.

And so, he knew damn well, had Bruno.

The roommates watched now, with mounting anxiety,
as the carriage of March's typewriter went whipsawing
back and forth, rolling up line after line of copy. Their
eyes met guiltily. While the two of them had spent the
morning hiding from the rain, rehashing stale releases
from the regimental public information office for their re-
spective papers, Adam March had been bird-dogging a
live story. It had to be a live one from the feverish way he
was working.

Hating themselves, but lacking both the will power and
self-respect to walk away, they crept closer and closer un-

til, finally, they were peering over his shoulder.

With his usual infallible timing, March looked up from his typewriter. Nothing could have pleased him more than to see the two of them there, caught red-faced, in the act.

"You're right, boys. It's a hot one all right. Just maybe the hottest item since the Tonkin Gulf. Stonewall has it for you—the briefing this afternoon—but I'll give it to you now. Fair is fair, right? You kept the place warm and cozy for me; I'll fill you in on my story." Smugly, he blew some more smoke at them. "Don't expect any telegrams of congratulations, though. I've already wired it back."

"To hell with you, Adam," Wharton sneered, turning away.

"Come on, Adam," Bruno said. He choked on his pride, but as always it went down. "What's the scoop?" March winked at Bruno, as if they had both been in on the gag that had Wharton so pissed off. Then he pushed himself out of the chair and moved jauntily over to a situation map thumbtacked onto the wall. It represented a broad area in the northwest corner of South Vietnam around Khesanh. He took a broad-tipped marking pen from his shirt pocket and scratched an "X" on the map above the besieged base near the demilitarized zone.

"For the past six months this sector has been policed by government troops," March explained. "It was pretty quiet up there until the North Vietnamese moved down in force. It didn't take more than a couple of battalions to do the job."

Wharton nodded. "I was up there just before Christmas. The SV troops are greenhorns. If I'm not mistaken," he said, looking to March, "they've got an American cadre."

"They do, indeed. A handful of officers and noncoms. Since the big Commie offensive, nobody knows too much what's been happening in the sector." He took a long, leisurely drag on his cigarette.

Bruno showed his impatience. "So, all right, Adam. For Chrissake!"

"So while you guys were sitting here, fanny to the fire, waiting for a handout to come and find you, I was up at the Rockpile snooping around their G-2 section."

"Sucking around, you mean," Wharton muttered.

March ignored him. "While I was there reconnoitering, a straggler from one of those South Vietnamese battalions dragged his ass into that outpost with a story that all of us are going to be involved with for quite a long time. Three days ago his outfit was hit hard by the Commies, really put through the meat grinder. Most of them that weren't killed took off into the jungle like scared bunnies. The American officers managed to rally about one hundred fifty men and fought their way clear."

"*That's* your big story?" Wharton said, obviously relieved. "So far I give you about a stick of type on page two. Tops."

March smiled. He was, they could see, enjoying himself immensely. "So far. . . . Only instead of heading south like the Reds expected, these one hundred and fifty men in the middle of enemy turf. . . ." His bright, lively eyes swung between Coleman and Bruno. "The senior American officer—a guy named David Walsh, remember that name, David Walsh—decided to raise a little hell. This Walsh, he took his commandoes all the way over here." He slashed the pen across the map and drew a dark circle touching the Laotian border. "And attacked a new airstrip Charley's been building on top of a mountain."

"Shit, Adam!" Wharton laughed harshly. "Where did you pick up that kind of a fairy tale? What in the *hell* would they want with an airstrip? To fly model planes on?"

"It's legit," March said evenly. His black eyes snapped with that total assurance. "You can check it out with Intelligence."

balls for them and a glass of ginger ale for Joshua.

Constance lifted her glass toward him. "I think the returning hero should make a toast."

"Hey, pop, yeah." The boy held his glass out too.

There was something about the solemnity of toasts that had always embarrassed Walsh, especially with his close friends and family. This was a solemn occasion, one of the most important moments, he knew, of his life. He would have wished to have been able to find the words to bind them all together with the moment and not have it lost in a few trite words. "To the new life. . . . To . . . uh . . . the brave new world."

"To our new life," his wife said with fervor. Her eyes watched him over the lip of the glass. "It is going to be like a new life for us, Dave," she said.

"Well, it's sure going to be different for the Negro GI when he comes home than it was after the last couple of wars. I want to talk to you about that, Connie."

"The black GI, pop," Joshua said.

He didn't understand.

"We don't say Negro any more," the boy explained. "We say black now." The arm shot out in what appeared to Dave to be a frightening imitation of a fascist salute, until he saw that Josh had only been, rather exuberantly, proposing a ginger ale toast. "To black power!" he said, his eyes gleaming with fierceness and pride.

"I'll drink to that, son," Walsh said. But he drank to it with mixed emotions. Joshua Walsh would be the first male of a long bloodline in many generations who would be truly proud of his black African ancestry. That was all to the good. Nothing could be more important. Fifteen years old. When Dave was fifteen he didn't know anything about the world beyond his own block. But the militant gleam disturbed him.

"We read a lot about black power over there," he said

cautiously. "I suppose it depends what you mean by it. The way some people mean it, it can be pretty dangerous stuff. Shooting, killing, that kind of power never solved any-body's problems. I found out the truth of that first hand. Where I just came from."

"That's Whitey's line pop, what he wants us to do. For him, anything goes." Joshua was explaining the facts of life to his father, quite patiently. He took a sip of the cold ginger ale. "Ain't nothing else gonna set us free. Ain't no-body gonna turn us around. They're afraid of us, pop. What-all we get is because they afraid we gonna burn 'em, like Watts. Gonna beat 'em. Whitey's afraid of us, pop. He gonna give us, 'cause he know he don' gonna give we gonna *take*."

During the harangue, which Dave could see was a repe-tition, probably word for word, from the things he had been hearing, Joshua had slowly slipped into The Accent, that combination of Southern drawl, mush-mouthed intel-ligibility, and northern stridency which had become the universal accent of the Negro slum kid.

Walsh gripped his glass tightly. Connie sent a signifi-cant look over to him, her lips pressed tightly together, as if to say, *You see what I've had to put up with.* Dave filled his lungs. When he did speak, he wanted to speak calmly. "You weren't taught to talk like that, Josh. You can talk civilized."

"Pop, I didn't. . . ." He was just a young kid again, looking pleadingly to his mother for help.

"Josh didn't mean anything, Dave," Constance said. You would hardly have believed this was the same woman who had just been pleading for help. "He's just a little boy talk-ing about things he doesn't quite understand. It's not the same as when we were coming up. There's so much going on in the world, and it's all in the papers and on television. We all get caught up in it, the young as well as the old. The kids speak out these days. They teach them to in school."

"Yeah, I guess." Dave slumped back into the chair. When he was coming up, they taught them that they were supposed to be seen, not heard. Did things, in fact, change for the better?

"I'm sorry, pop," Josh said. He had a wide-mouthed, crooked, very appealing smile. "I'm always mouthing off, ask ma."

"You don't have to apologize. You've got opinions, you got a right to express them. If you can't express them here in your own home, where can you?"

The boy, disappointed in the father, was willing to tell himself that he was wrong. The father, astonished by the boy, and a little afraid, was unwilling to let him see how astonished and how afraid.

"How did we ever get off on such a somber subject anyway," Constance wanted to know. "What I said about a new life, I meant the *Walsh's* new life."

"It's not going to be all that different, Connie." Finishing his drink, he immediately poured himself a fresh one. "A schoolteacher is a schoolteacher. Even with a Union."

"Oh, Dave, stop it." She went over to the couch and sat down close up against him. Her hand found his, fingers entwining. "I'm glad if your suits won't fit you. I like you in uniform, don't you, Josh?"

"You look great, pop!" he exclaimed, the political theorist having given way for the moment to the young boy who had a soldier for a father.

Walsh was frowning down at his wife. "That's not what you said when I was called back."

"Or what I would say if you were going back now. But that's all over now. And, Davie, it did work out wonderfully. I can hardly believe it. I'm so proud of you, Dave."

"Don't be too proud."

"I was so excited I couldn't sleep all night waiting for

today." Joshua got down on his knees by the coffee table and refilled his glass with ginger ale.

Constance laughed. "Oh, no! *He* couldn't sleep. I came in at midnight to check his covers, and he was gone to the world. And that's the last of that before supper, young man."

"I must have woke up later then," the boy insisted. "I really couldn't, pop. I kept seeing those pictures in the paper and thinking, that's my father . . . that's my pop!"

Constance moved away from him, sitting with her legs drawn up underneath her on the cushions so that she could look at him.

"You better stay in your uniform anyway, Dave. Your father is coming over." She took a deep breath. "And Lester and Miriam."

Walsh groaned. His head fell back unhappily. "Can't you stall them off for another day or two? I'm tired. I want to get acquainted with you two again."

Constance was defensive. "Well, they are family. You can't blame them for wanting to see their hero. Lester and Miriam are flying in from Hollywood. What could I say to them, Dave?"

"Hollywood?" Walsh sighed. "It figures."

"Lester's firm is handling the public relations on a big TV spectacular to raise funds for the BWB."

"BWB? That's a new one on me."

"The Black and White Brotherhood Committee. Harry Belafonte is going to be on it. Sammy Davis, Jr., Ed Sullivan, almost everyone you can name."

"Aunt Miriam is taking this real big, pop," Joshua said.

"I can imagine. Miriam with Harry Belafonte and Ed Sullivan. The crowning moment of her career."

"Not that," Joshua said. "*You.*"

Walsh looked to his wife. "How come?"

"You know how Miriam is, Dave. She and Lester read

about it in *The Los Angeles Times,* and she's been calling me every hour on the hour ever since to find out when you were coming back. You know how infantile she is about celebrities, even if they so much as step on her toes." Her face lit up with satisfaction. "I can just see her running around the TV studio, telling everybody that you're her brother-in-law."

"I'll bet that impresses Harry and Sammy," he said.

"Honestly, Dave, I don't know what it is with you that you have to tear yourself down. I mean, what did you expect? Your own father, I should think you'd want to see him. And, ready or not, Miriam *is* my sister."

"And Lester *is* my brother-in-law. My rich and successful brother-in-law." He glanced sharply at Joshua, "Who made it big with brain power. Not black power or gun power, but brain power."

Josh seemed about to say something but, thinking better of it, cast his eyes down to show that he was properly ashamed of himself or, at least, didn't want any more arguing.

Constance had stretched out her arm and was caressing the back of his neck with her soft fingers. "I just want to show you off, hon. Is that so selfish of me?"

Her touch, the love in her soft eyes, melted him. "I don't mind my old man, he's all right." It wasn't seeing people he minded, anyway; it was just that he didn't feel up to talking to them. "Maybe Lester will get lost in a crap game or something. Maybe his plane will be grounded."

Very seriously, Joshua said, "It never rains in Los Angeles, pop." He tapped his head, indicating brain power, and beamed when both his parents roared.

They thought they knew everything, these kids. Well, Joshua knew one hell of a lot more than he had known at fifteen. And that was putting it mildly.

"Then it looks as if I am trapped by a meteorological

phenomenon. Nothing short of a race rumble in the Black and White Brotherhood Committee can keep them from getting here." He reached across the table and rumpled the boy's short kinky hair.

If Dave didn't really want to see them, he got a short reprieve. Miriam phoned Constance from Kennedy Airport to let her know they weren't going to be able to make it in time for supper. Lester had been called to his boss's apartment for a very important conference. She had then insisted on having Constance put Dave on the phone so she could tell him personally how proud she was of him.

"I'm gonna want to know all about it, lover," she told him. "Every gruesome detail. And you know me well enough to know I'm not kidding. I'm gonna pump you dry. It kills me we've got to come so late, but you know what they say: if I'm not there, lover, start without me."

"A very important conference," Connie said, after he had hung up. "That doesn't sound like so much." Dave frowned at her for a moment and then he remembered that it was a running joke between them that Lester Sampson tended to run to hyperbole. They had once even worked out a trip to the men's room for Lester in which each of the necessary actions could be described by his favorite words: "top level," "ultra crucial," and his favorite word of all, "fabulous."

For years, the standing joke between Walsh and Constance was that Lester was the "black man in the gray flannel suit," and when they finally told him about it, he had arranged a write-up in the advertising news pages of *The New York Times* under that heading.

Although Walsh had always regarded his brother-in-law as a little bit of a phoney, he had to admire him for his courage and ambition. Lester Sampson had been in the front ranks of the miniscule force of Negroes who had an anonymous well-wisher.

Leaning back, crossing his skinny legs, Amos began to tell his grandson one of the stories they had all heard so many times that Constance, standing behind his chair, rolled her eyes upward and hurried into the kitchen.

The story, which concerned his days as a Pullman porter on the once celebrated Twentieth Century Limited from New York to Los Angeles was hardly calculated to gain either the attention or respect of a 15-year-old boy who was all out to take what Whitey had with a gun. Walsh studied his son's face with mounting apprehension. Josh's lips were not quite smiling. It was impossible to tell whether it was subdued amusement or patient contempt.

Walsh was relieved when the door chimes broke in.

"You get it, will you, honey," Constance shouted. "I'm up to my elbow in here. Joshua, come hopping."

Walsh walked around behind his father's chair, stopping to startle the old man with a quick, gruff hug of the shoulders. He paused in the vestibule before the door for a moment, his hands at his sides, girding himself. The chimes sounded again. Sighing heavily he reached for the knob.

David Walsh would have died before saying it, but his wife Constance seemed plain alongside her younger sister Miriam. Both women had slender figures, good features, the same light, flawless complexions. They were unmistakably sisters. It was only when he was confronted by Miriam's perfection—and perfection was the word—that Walsh was aware that Constance had any imperfections at all. But there was more to it than physical appeal, more even than stylishness, polish, or dress. Miriam crackled with life; she hit like a whirlwind; she was a dynamo of energy and fun.

Taking the initiative as always, she ran to Walsh, her heels clicking rat-a-tat on the floor, kissed him on the mouth, then on the cheek, and then, wetly, on the ear. "You

great big wonderful doll you!" she bubbled, overflowing
with emotion. "Oh, Dave, you're just too much. Too, too
much!"

She had a way of bringing out the best of people. She
could make even Dave, who would be the first to admit
that he was a rather dull fellow, feel like a gay dog.

Dave hugged her back, laughing a little self-con-
sciously. "*That* I like! What do you say you go back outside
and we'll play it over again?"

He swung her around to one side with his left arm
around her waist, as if they were doing a dance break so
that he could greet Lester who was standing just inside the
doorway, his hands folded in front of himself patiently.
Lester Sampson was a good-looking man in his late thirties; stocky, shorter than his wife in her spiked heels, and of
a much darker complexion. He wore the easy, self-assured,
well-tailored look of success. Shaking hands, he covered
Dave's own hand with both of his in a sudden extra gesture
of warmth.

"Les, it's really great to see you," Walsh told him, re-
sponding quite naturally to that kind of enthusiasm. "I
don't know that I'd recommend flying back from Hollywood just to welcome me home, but I'm glad you did."

"You lie," Miriam said. She placed her own hand over
his. "You couldn't wait to get your hands on me. Tell him,
Les. We would have walked back to New York if that was
the only way. We would have crawled."

The way Les was looking at him, affectionate and
pleased, showed that he was agreeing with her. "Man, you
sure look great. The Army must agree with you."

Lester himself had put on weight. Walsh tapped the
younger man's middle and grinned.

"Want me to see if I can fix it up for you, Les?"

Lester pulled back his head and sucked in his cheeks.
"Much as I would like to oblige the U. S. Army in its cur-

pulsive and uncommon display of emotion toward his brother-in-law, he came up behind Dave and gripped his arms tightly.

"Dave, you old SOB, Miriam's right. We're all so darned proud of you, we could bust. You did it, fella. You really did it."

Walsh had all he could do not to cringe. Not to tighten up and pull away.

"Les," he said with a good humor he did not feel, "how about opening that case on the floor and digging out a couple of bottles of that cheap fizz juice you sent us."

The kitchen wall clock read five minutes before midnight when Walsh opened the fifth bottle of champagne. The cacaphony of voices, high with gaiety, happily intoxicated, funneled through the dining room to him. He leaned against the sink for a moment and pressed the cold green bottle against his throbbing forehead.

"I still think you were crazy to run out on the show to rush back here," Constance was saying for the tenth time. "Dave is going to be around for a while."

Lester chuckled. "So is Hollywood. I got to admit, though, that place is fabulous. I don't like to use that word, but no other word will possibly do. Absolutely fabulous. But then that husband of yours is a little fabulous too."

Walsh groaned.

"You think Hollywood is something today?" he heard his father say. "You should have seen it in the Thirties. Then it was really something, let me tell you. . . . I was on that New York to L. A. run then. I had that run for five years, Lester. . . ."

"Pop," Miriam hooted. "Back in those days they wouldn't let *you* out of the railyards unless it was to walk Mary Pickford's dog."

"Mary Pickford?" Lester said. "Mary Pickford? How old

is this girl, anyway? You sure this is your *kid* sister,
Connie?"

"Oh, oh," Miriam said, "I feel the dagger eyes of old
Black and Beautiful."

Picturing the scene in his mind, Walsh could see them
too. The old jokes, he was learning, didn't go with these
wild kids, burning in their juices.

"Well, black is the beautiful color in the entertainment
business," Lester said smugly. "Would you believe that the
agencies can't find enough black talent to meet the de-
mands of television? Did you think you'd live to see the
day, pop?"

"How about Aunt Miriam?" Joshua asked. "She's got it
all over Diahann Carroll any day."

Dave heard a high, female whoop. "For that I am going
to raise you to the exalted rank of Afro-American and give
you a big sloppy kiss." There was the sound of running
feet, followed by Joshua's unconvincing protestings and
gigglings. "In another year you won't be struggling,"
Miriam said. "From what I hear, the white girls ask the
black boys for it now. Is that right?"

Immediately, there arose some mild, embarrassed pro-
tests from both Lester and Constance.

"He could teach us all," Miriam said. "They got to do
more than ask," she said. "Make 'em pay you, Josh-u-ay."

"All right," Constance announced. "It's getting late.
Josh. . . ."

Dave had decided that he had better get in there and
help his wife out. Her face was just about what he had expected it to be, stiff and disapproving. "It's twelve o'clock,
Joshua. I think you had better say good night to your aunt
and uncle and get off to bed."

"Awwww, mom!"

"And in celebration of your father's homecoming, let's
see if you can do it without any arguments."

Miriam sniffed. "Hard-hearted Hannah. Don't worry, lover. Dear old Auntie Miriam will sneak in later with a fifth of champagne, and we'll have ourselves a party." She held out her empty glass to Dave. "It's about time! What were you doing, bottling it?"

Lester shook his head while Walsh refilled his glass. "This kid of yours. He gets bigger every time I see him."

"Now there's an original observation," Miriam said, "The creative mind at work."

Lester smiled foolishly. "You see how it's been going, Josh. This isn't *my* night at all."

Walsh roughed up his son's hair. The kid's argument had been purely perfunctory. He was out on his feet. "You kiss your mother and grandpa and get to bed."

Lester put his hand over his glass. "Don't let me have any more of this stuff, Dave. I'm on the wagon, but this is a special occasion." He rubbed his stomach. "The bland diet."

Amos Walsh leaned forward and inspected Lester's paunch with new respect. "No joke about show business and ulcers, eh, Lester?"

"They put it in your contract now, pop," Lester said with a hint of condescension.

Walsh reached for his father's glass, but the old man covered it with his hand. "No more for me, son. I'll hold out for the coffee and cake later."

With an elaborate dignity that made Walsh smile, Lester removed a cigar from the pocket of his vest and studied it for imperfections. He lit it, finally, and leaned back in his chair, puffing thoughtfully.

"Dave . . . my motives in rushing back to New York from the Coast were neither purely familial nor entirely altruistic." He used both words with obvious pride.

"Don't get 'familial' with me," Miriam muttered. "But I'll take all the 'altruistic' you can dish out." Miriam was,